TwentyWhen?

Somewhere Between Heaven And Hell

Scott Millar

BALBOA.
PRESS

A DIVISION OF HAY HOUSE

Balboa Press books may be ordered through booksellers or by contacting:

Balboa Press
A Division of Hay House
1663 Liberty Drive
Bloomington, IN 47403
www.balboapress.com
1-(877) 407-4847

Because of the dynamic nature of the Internet, any web addresses or links contained in this book may have changed since publication and may no longer be valid. The views expressed in this work are solely those of the author and do not necessarily reflect the views of the publisher, and the publisher hereby disclaims any responsibility for them.

The author of this book does not dispense medical advice or prescribe the use of any technique as a form of treatment for physical, emotional, or medical problems without the advice of a physician, either directly or indirectly. The intent of the author is only to offer information of a general nature to help you in your quest for emotional and spiritual well-being. In the event you use any of the information in this book for yourself, which is your constitutional right, the author and the publisher assume no responsibility for your actions.

Any people depicted in stock imagery provided by Thinkstock are models, and such images are being used for illustrative purposes only.
Certain stock imagery © Thinkstock.

ISBN: 978-1-4525-4458-8 (sc)
ISBN: 978-1-4525-4459-5 (e)
Library of Congress Control Number: 2011963457
Printed in the United States of America

Balboa Press rev. date:2/06/2012

FOR BRENDAN AND SALLY.

Without their tireless help and encouragement this book
would never have become a reality.

FOR MY WIFE SHAYNE

With grateful thanks for understanding I had to write this
book, and for putting up with my frequent distractions.

Preface

This little parable came about when I had been to church more than three-thousand times before coming to the conclusion God did not exist.

At about the same time I began to study evolution, and quickly realised that the Bible story of how our planet Earth, including its fauna and flora, was formed is simply untrue, though with underlying similarities.

The essential point of divergence lay around the use of the word "day" in Genesis, telling Christians God made their world in six days, and rested on the seventh.

Through my travels around Christianity and Evolution I gradually realised they were not mutually exclusive, and that God probably planned evolution in the beginning.

Acknowledgements

Of course the Christian Bible exists, as does the book The Little World of Don Camillo by Giovanni Guareschi. Winston Curchill's quote is genuine, and Charles Darwin's thoughts are well-known by some. Martin Luther existed, as did the various Popes mentioned.

I have used some information found in World Religions by Debbie Gill, and from The Catholic Church by Hans Kung. Allan Wilson is real, as are the British Royal Family.

Apart from these, the characters in my parable are purely imaginary.

Mary And Matthew

Excerpt from the Diary of Mary Collins, Chicago, Illinois, dated 9th February, 1988.

I spoke to God for the first time today, and I'm still shivering with excitement. When I told Mom and Pop they seemed sceptical.

I was surprised and awed, because I never really believed it was possible.

As I knelt by my bed after saying the Lord's Prayer, I had this strange feeling somebody had come silently into my bedroom. I looked around, but there was nobody there. I peered into my mirror from where I knelt, seeing only big blue eyes wide with excitement, a small freckled nose, and my pale white face framed by its straw-coloured fringe.

I closed my eyes again to start prayers for my twin brother Brad, then heard what seemed like wind blowing through trees, grass rustling, and a voice inside my head, I mean, not coming in through my ears like other sounds do, saying to me, "Mary, your twin brother Brad is here with me in Heaven. Speak to him now."

I was thinking Thank you, God, Thank you, then held my breath as I heard Brad's voice, calm and happy. He said Mom, Pop, and I shouldn't blame him for the accident, even though he'd driven the car after drinking vodka at our sixteenth birthday party.

Brad told me he can see us from Heaven, where everything is beautiful and peaceful, everyone is happy, and if he just thinks of songs or music he likes, he hears them immediately.

When I asked Brad what God looked like, he replied he couldn't see God, but knew He was always there right beside him.

'And you too, Mary,' God told me.

Now that I know we can keep in touch, I'll be a much better person, 'cos I won't do anything God and Brad don't approve of.

Excerpt from the Diary of Matthew Draper, Cape Town, South Africa, dated 9th February, 1988.

I spoke to God last night!!! Can hardly believe it! Got the idea to try from the book Dad and Mum gave me a week ago for my sixteenth birthday called 'The Little World of Don Camillo'.

Don Camillo is a Catholic priest in a small Italian town which has a Communist Mayor who regularly hassles him. During frequent conversations with God, Don often asks His help in outwitting the Mayor, but doesn't always get the advice he hopes for. I suppose I won't either.

Talking to God was much easier than I thought it would be.

After saying The Lord's Prayer kneeling by my bed like I always do, I just asked God if I could talk to Him, and He answered in a voice which sounded as though it was blown by a gentle breeze across shimmering water towards me, telling me I could speak to Him whenever I felt the need to, because He's always near me.

So I asked God to please help Dad and Mum get over their problems, like shouting at each other, then not talking for days on end, and sleeping in separate rooms.

God said He would help them through me if I can't convince them they can also speak to Him. When Dad gets back from his business trip to Jo'burg on Saturday I'm going to speak to them.

God, thanks to your inspiration I scored an 86-ball century against Rondebosch Boys High today. The coach said I never played a careless shot, but I know YOU inspired me to achieve it.

Thank you, God. I love you. Goodnight. M.

Excerpt from the Diary of Mary Collins, Chicago, Illinois, dated 9th February, 1989.

Today is the first anniversary of speaking to God and Brad in Heaven. As usual, after saying hello to God and asking His forgiveness for anything I'd done which He might not approve of, and reminding Him I love Him, He said 'Here is Brad to speak to you.'

My twin brother told me there are no birthdays or anniversaries there.

I asked him if people get older in Heaven, 'cos if they don't and I die when I'm eighty, Brad will still be only sixteen when we meet again.

He replied that in Heaven, age means nothing, like time.

I'm so glad.

I told him that I've been trying all year to convince Mom and Pop that I speak to God and Brad, but they still tell me they often try but don't get through.

Excerpt from the Diary of Matthew Draper, Kenilworth, Cape Town, dated 8th January 1989.

Tonight is my first anniversary of talking to God.

Together we've been able to get Dad and Mum back on the right track, even though neither of them is able to actually talk to God like I can.

They started by becoming good friends again, since when it's just got better and better.

God helped me twice in class today. First, by suggesting I try the word serpent in the translation of an English essay about a snake into French. It was right and I scored 83%. Then He helped me to finally understand what Pythagoras Theorem actually means, and its simple practical application of describing a perfect right-angle on any flat surface, so for the first time I'm starting to feel confident about passing Matric next year.

Thank You, God. I love you. Goodnight. M.

Excerpt from the Diary of Mary Collins, Chicago, Illinois, Dated 9th January, 1990.

Today is the second anniversary of me talking to Brad and God.

Brad told me he approves of my boyfriend Mark Lincoln, tho' we met for the first time at my birthday party last week. Brad said I mustn't feel bad about Mark dropping Kim for me, as we are obviously meant for each other, so now I feel REALLY HAPPY AND SO PROUD!!!..........that I will dream of Mark again tonight.

Excerpt from the Diary of Matthew Draper, Kenilworth, Cape Town, 8th February, 1990.

Tonight is my second anniversary of talking to God.

Dad and Mum continue to go from strength to strength, and next Sunday they're going to church to rededicate their marriage vows.

I got my Matric results today, with distinctions in English, French, and Mathematics.

Dad and Mum are taking me and six of my friends to celebrate at the Brass Bell for dinner on Friday evening. Wow!

God, without your help I wouldn't have achieved one distinction, never mind three.

You remember how upset I was when my Housemaster wrote to Dad and Mum last year to warn them I was unlikely to achieve a pass. You told me to work and concentrate harder, and I would prove him wrong. You were right, and I will be going to the University of Cape Town in three weeks. Alleluia!!

I love you, God. Goodnight. M.

Last undated entry from the Diary of Mary Collins, Chicago, Illinois.

I'm shattered that I've had no communications with God or Brad for longer than a month now.

What have I done wrong? Nothing I can think of. My pleading prayers go unanswered, but I'll keep trying. It seems like the end of my world. I wonder if Armageddon is coming soon? I really, really hope not.

Last undated entry from the Diary of Matthew Draper, Kenilworth, Cape Town.

For some reason I cannot understand, God has just stopped talking to me. There's only silence after I say The Lord's Prayer and try and talk to Him.

I'm going to continue trying, but I've got this feeling it won't work anymore.

Maybe God thinks I don't need Him because I'm at university now.

After all, there are millions of people all over the world who probably need his help much more than I do, so I mustn't be selfish.

If you read this, God, please understand that I understand, and will always love You, God. Goodnight. M.

Mary

Our Christmas church service finally over, I took Mark's warm hand as we were swept relentlessly towards where Pastor Mick Warner stood tall at The Crux's ornate exit, God's blonde shepherd beaming a benevolent smile of impossibly even white teeth on his happily fleeced flock.

Six thousand five hundred worshippers, not counting those who'd gladly stood in wide aisles for the opening of Chicago's The New Timber Bay Congregation Church of the Crux and its adjoining, sprawling, already busy business complex.

Pastor Warner, since his extended sabbatical resembling some human amalgam of Schwarzenegger, Stallone, and Billy Graham, briefly raised a fluttering right hand to bestow a small spark of recognition upon us regulars.

Like a shoal of captured fish our congregation quickly disgorged from the net of The Crux's vast new amphitheatre, heading for banks, gyms, food court, and shopping mall.

I urgently needed pills for a splitting headache, and after a bewildering five-minute walk during which we glanced momentarily into a frantic child-care centre, and a gym the size of an aircraft hangar where patrons were already pumping iron and jogging treadmills, we thankfully entered Chicago's newest, largest drugstore, where I asked an African-American assistant dressed in a sky-blue THE NEW CRUX uniform for my requirements, including a glass of water.

'Mary, after you please, sweetheart.' Mark pleaded, agitatedly massaging his brow with the fingers of both hands.

Another five-minute walk in the gradually thinning crowd brought us to our car, parked in lot number 4017.

Sighing in unison we got in thankfully, shaking our heads in astonishment at what we'd experienced during the last ninety mind-blowing minutes.

'Mary', Mark exclaimed, insinuating his long, lithe frame into the Mustang's driver seat, and pushing curly light brown hair away from dark hazel eyes which he aimed at me before continuing, 'Pastor Mick Warner's had more than a face-lift, he's had a character change as well! Did you hear that guy next to me referring to him as a "pastorpreneur"? What's more,' Mark added before I could answer, 'he seemed to say it with a sense of pride!'

I replied that I hadn't, actually, but in light of what we'd seen, heard, and experienced this Christmas morning, it seemed rather apt.

The opening of The New Timber Bay Congregation Church of the Crux had been timed to coincide with Christmas Day, 'Simultaneously celebrating the birth of Jesus Christ and The New Crux,' Mick Warner, arms raised and spread wide had announced from his lectern on stage through the surround-sound system, his beautifully modulated voice resonating effortlessly in every part of the blue-domed amphitheatre.

Above and behind him, on the ultra-wide two-thousand four hundred square feet video screen, the congregation avidly watched scenes of the nativity, then three-dimensional visuals from the design and construction phases of this enormous new monument to God.

At one point Warner took the opportunity to promote his latest book, God's Assignment, thirty million copies sold and still counting, the proceeds from which, he informed rapt listeners, was going to 'Freeing Sudanese Slaves in Darfur. Let's all become active emancipators.' This revelation and exhortation had elicited a standing ovation, and brought tears to the eyes of many.

How I longed for the "old" Crux days, when Mick's father Bill was our pastor in a simple little stone church, which we passed just before turning into our driveway.

Back home, Mark and I changed into casual clothes to suit unseasonably mild winter weather, and carried steaming mugs of coffee onto our timber deck overlooking southern Lake Michigan, where several small boats with brightly-coloured sails had detached themselves from a forest of yacht masts and were enjoying a gentle southerly breeze.

As usual after a church service, its sermon was our first subject for discussion. Did we feel enlightened or enriched in any way?

Unsurprisingly, this Christmas morning Warner had selected the first two chapters of Genesis as reference for his theme of beginnings.

Now, Mark and I've been going to church together since we first met on my eighteenth birthday. But I feel I never, ever, want to go to The New Crux again after our experience there this morning.

Together we've quite recently come to doubt some of Christianity's teachings, and where it all started is the Bible story of how God made our world, and how that description seems completely and utterly at odds with what science has so far revealed about the origins of our planet in general, and evolution in particular.

And we're not talking 'micro-evolution' here. We believe evolution to be fact, including the evolution of humankind.

Much of evolution is just plain common sense anyway, we've realised now, but I guess common sense isn't as common as it should be! In addition to that, Allan Wilson's work effectively shows every human alive today to be a living fossil. The list goes on.

My mind had been constantly returning to this concern as Pastor (Pastorpreneur?--the newly-coined word has a certain ring of truth to it,) Mick Warner's sermon progressed.

Mark and I, partners in our own law firm as we are in life, understand only too well how whole issues in law can turn on the reading of a single word. Christianity's Bible is no different, and I was itching to test an idea that germinated in my head by the end of Warner's sermon.

As Mark rose to refill our coffee mugs, I did too, and brought a Reader's Digest Oxford Complete Wordfinder from our library, which I placed on his lap with an enigmatic smile.

He looked up at me quizzically, and smiled too. After nineteen years, Mark's smile still makes my heart miss a beat, and Mark smiles at me twenty times a day. Eat your heart out, Mr Pastorpreneur Schwarzenneger /Stallone/ Billy Graham!

'What's all this about, sweetheart?' Mark sipped his coffee, opened the heavy book speculatively about halfway, and pushed his lean frame upright in anticipation of something interesting developing.

'It could be all about different meanings of the word "day",' I replied, pulling my chair up next to his, peering intently at the pages as my husband turned them, as only someone who spends much of their lives reading and referring to books does, with care and consideration. So do I, I reminded myself.

Quickly scanning the appropriate text with a practiced eye, I registered the words----the time between sunrise and sunset---a period of twenty-four hours as a unit of time, esp. from midnight to midnight, corresponding to a complete revolution of the earth on its axis---age---period---era---epoch---date---time---lifetime, amongst numerous others.

'Time next, please Hon. The word "time".' Nearly three columns, but there among many others appeared the same words, ---age---period---epoch---era--lifetime.

I gave Mark's shoulder a squeeze, saying with a touch of excitement, 'I've got what I want, thanks Hon.' Nodding his head in dawning understanding of the implications of what we'd just read, Mark said with real conviction, 'We, in fact everyone who reads The Bible, are taking it too literally, aren't we.' It was a statement, not a question. Mark gently closed the dictionary, and put his hand on mine, while I waited expectantly for his follow-up.

'If, instead of the word "day" in Genesis to describe what God did for six of them to form our world, the scribes who wrote Genesis, or those who later interpreted, translated, or edited it had used "age", "era", "epoch", or "period" instead, for instance, then Genesis-the first book of Moses- would begin to make sense with what we now know of how long it took for our planet to become what it is, and of evolution too, wouldn't it." Another simple statement, one with which I agreed wholeheartedly.

I was really getting into this discussion now, feeling a deep sense of relief and quickly growing excitement that our accumulating doubts about the veracity of some Christian teachings could be allayed by a simple re-interpretation of its Bible, hardly an original concept in the history of Christianity, I know.

After all, comparisons between contemporary English versions of the Bible and older versions reveal significant differences.

> My King James 1957 version states, *inter alia,* and I went
> to check now exactly what it said:
> The Old And New Testaments Translated out of the
> original tongues and with the former translations diligently
> compared and revised   …….For when Your Highness had
> once, out of deep judgement, apprehended how convenient
> it was, that, out of the original Sacred Tongues, together
> with comparing of the labours, both in our own and other
> foreign languages, of many worthy men who went before
> us, there would be one more exact translation of the Holy
> Scriptures into the *English* tongue; ….

Talk about labours! How laboured is that English of the time of King James not that long ago!

I returned to the deck with this Bible, and found the beginning of Genesis, which starts so promisingly for Christian believers of evolution. "In the beginning God created the heaven and the earth."

Mark broke into my chain of thought by asking, 'To what extent does Christianity preclude theologians and educators from exercising common sense and reality in their mission to inform and enlighten about our planet and its life forms? Aren't they blinded to reality by their religion? Shouldn't morality keep pace with technology?'

I answered 'Yes, yes, and yes!' as we picked up our things and moved inside, the mild Christmas-day weather beginning to deteriorate noticeably now, Chicago living up to its nickname of "The Windy City", with sailboats already heading back to harbour, and took our customary seats at the large circular cedar-wood dining table.

I was reminded of what Winston Churchill once said, that "No-one should look down on those honourable, well meaning people who gave their time and lives wholeheartedly to the betterment of our lives.

" Much is coming to light about our planet and its history. It is therefore important to rely upon authentic discovery and revelation, despite that these may be at cross-purposes to our upbringing and training."

Mark continued, 'Mary, we aren't the first Christian believers in God to think like this. We can't be. It's simply that we've had it drummed into us, since before we could read, or think for ourselves, that the Bible is the unalterable Word of God. Learn now, understand later.' Mark rose as he said this, gave my shoulder a loving squeeze, and explained he was fetching reference books from our library.

I leant forward and drew the antique globe towards me from the centre of the table, slowly turning it so that the area now generally referred to as the Middle East, and the birth-place of Jesus Christ over two millennia ago, was facing me.

This was where Christianity began during the time of the Roman Empire. Not far away in Egypt, and three thousand years earlier, that country's inhabitants had built pyramids and numerous other structures which are a source of awe and wonder to this day, could write and read, and worshipped numerous part-animal, part-human gods representing natural forces, such as the river Nile.

'How long did the Bible as we know it now take to write, sweetheart?' my husband enquired as he slid back into his chair beside mine, and laid two Bibles, one new and one old, plus a History of The World's Religions in front of him.

'A thousand years, give or take', I answered, adding 'and in a variety of languages based around Aramaic, the language of Syria from about the sixth century, Hebrew, and Greek. And let's not forget the Bible was heavily edited, Hon.'

'How do we know that?' Mark enquired, eyebrows raised questioningly.

'Well, apart from anything else, there are a number of gospels which weren't included. The books of The Apocrypha, from the Greek word "hidden", were written later than the rest of The Old Testament, and included in the old Greek translation of The Bible.

'Then Martin Luther came along and deleted the Apocrypha from the Reformation Bible, so they remain controversial in the Protestant Church to this day, so are seldom or ever mentioned.

'For all we know more may be discovered in future.

' Much history critical of the Old Testament, which represents seventy percent of our Bible, was confiscated over decades and centuries by Popes and others, so crushing unwelcome biblical research before it could take root. In any case, the Bible only describes, could only describe, let's face it, what was known to its scribes and editors of the world around them, no doubt suitably embellished by tales of travellers. We now know much was going on well outside of this extremely limited area of knowledge and hearsay.

'Their scope of human experience was not related in any way to the history of our planet.'

'They'd no doubt have believed the earth was flat, too, wouldn't they?' Mark interjected before adding, 'and they describe God as having human form, or at least of making humans "in His image". Can we truly believe God is human? If you asked the majority of mankind who believe in the God Christians, Muslims, and others do, they would undoubtedly think of Him as a wise old man with a white beard somewhere high above them, wherever they are, probably in Heaven. And where or what is Heaven, I wonder, but I don't expect you to answer that, sweetheart.'

'No doubt,' I agreed before continuing, 'in the 1850's, I'm sure it was, the immaculate conception of Mary without original sin became an immutable dogma promulgated by Pope Pius IX, certain of his own infallibility, despite that no Biblical reference to it was made in the previous thousand years. And let's not forget he received beatification at the start of this millennium!'

The information I'd studied quite recently kept flooding my mind, Mark was listening attentively, so I continued, 'Oh! And by the way,' 'this dogma of Pius IX was promulgated in the same decade Charles Darwin announced his theory, having kept it under wraps for two decades because of his wife's beliefs, until he had it published as ' The Origin of Species by Means of Natural Selection' in 1859, knowing others were about to beat him to it. "D'you know where Darwin's remains were interred, Hon?' I enquired a bit mischievously.

But with aplomb and a grin Hon quickly answered 'Westminster Abbey!' followed by the question, "the word Bible itself derives from the Greek word simply meaning 'the books, right?'

I answered affirmatively before continuing, 'Bear in mind too, Hon, the Jesus movement, for He never spoke in public about founding a church, became Church of the Roman Empire in the fourth century.

'In fact a much later Pope, Pius XII, considered Christ was a Roman and Jews responsible for murdering God. And he's a Pope who once negotiated a concordat with Adolf Hitler, believe it or not, but I digress!'

My husband waded in, saying emphatically, 'Sweetheart, we know Christianity's past has been violent and deceitful. It has thrived on allusions, delusions, illusions. And let's not forget literally millions of women were burned at the stake during the Inquisition, the reason why there are no female Catholic priests or rabbis to this day,' he finished indignantly.

Picking up the World's Religions, I found the Christianity section, and flipped pages to follow what I was after.

'From Christianity's well documented history, we must remind ourselves once more that controversies surrounding the relationship between Jesus Christ, God, and man caused several schisms in the Christian Church between the third and seventh centuries.

'The Great Schism of 1054 finally split the church into Eastern Christendom and Western Christendom.

Mark interjected, 'And how many more schisms would there have been if evolution had been part of the equation?'

I nodded ruefully before continuing, 'And these were followed by the Mediaeval Inquisition in 1231, the Spanish Inquisition exactly two-and-a-half centuries later, a fifteenth century Renaissance, a third Inquisition, a Reformation and a Counter Revolution in the sixteenth and seventeenth centuries.'

'Wow! And of course that wasn't the end of conflict and division either,' exclaimed Mark as I paused for a sip of water before continuing,

'No, far from it. Christianity split into the Roman Catholic Church, Protestantism, and Humanism.

'Protestantism, effectively bestowing upon its adherents the right to interpret the Bible in their own way, split into Church of England, Calvinism, and Lutherism, after which the Church of England fragmented into Noncomformists, Baptists, Methodists, Evangelicals, Congregationalists, Modernists, etcetera.

I noticed Mark stroking his chin in some astonishment.

'You see, Hon, obviously what started as Christ's simple creed, in which the formation of a church apparently didn't feature, was soon complicated and contaminated by the many different ways in which Christians later interpreted it.'

'Talk about change,' my man muttered.

'I mean, Hon, the mind starts to boggle, doesn't it, at how many different Bible interpretations, in every meaning of that word, were probably dished out by all and sundry during those massive and frequent religious upheavals? In fact, that trend continues to this day with all our various modern Bibles.

'And on top of all that, we both know how difficult the English language is to master. I mean, words which sound the same, like r-a-i-n, r-e-i-g-n, r-e-i-n, for instance, have different meanings, and there're thousands like that. A word can be a noun or a verb, like run, and fish. Read, as we know, can be present or past tense, depending on how it's pronounced.

'Kiss!' Mark added, winking suggestively, so I did.

Really into my stride now I continued this theme, Mark's eyes never leaving mine as he continued nodding in thoughtful agreement.

'I believe William Shakespeare personally invented over fifteen hundred words which are in common use today.

'Idioms comprise words whose meaning can't be understood from the words themselves.' I took a sip of soda. 'As in "feeling under the weather."

I gather there's a town in Bulgaria whose Cyrillic spelling can be--- I paused momentarily---transliterated, I believe that's the word, seven different ways. The potential for misunderstandings or different interpretations, deliberate or otherwise, in most languages is endless.'

Following my train of thought precisely, Mark mentioned what profound effects punctuation too has on the meanings of phrases or sentences containing the same words, giving a quick example 'Go, get him doctors. Go get him, doctors. And let me show you this one.'

Gently sliding the old Book towards him, Mark soon found what he was looking for, another example in St. Matthew. 'I remember well,' he told me, characteristically combing his hair with long slender fingers, 'how confused I was when I first read this in Matthew: "The book of the origin of Jesus Christ, the son of David, the son of Abraham." Even then, in my mind, I moved the commas around so the sentence read: "The book of the origin of Jesus Christ the son, of David the son of Abraham." Did the Bible mean Abraham was Christ's grandfather? Or that David was Abraham's son? Or were any of them even related? I still wonder reading it now. Of course there were, though the Bible only explains this later, fourteen generations separating Abraham and David.

'Do Hebrew and Greek use such things as commas, I wonder?' Mark muttered, but I wasn't sure and shrugged, so he continued, 'Let's not forget too, sweetheart, how emphasis placed on a particular word in a sentence may significantly alter that sentence's meaning. Now this new Bible,' Mark closed one and opened the other, 'will leave no doubt, as it's been "modernised", of course.' Stroking his chin again thoughtfully, he paused before going on, 'Modern writers and editors may well have put their own spin on it, or done so at someone's suggestion, insistence, even threat, perhaps. And,' Mark added in agitation, suddenly getting up and prowling round the table with long, deliberate strides, 'The scribes who wrote the books comprising our Bible could have had no notion,' he slashed the air with his hand, 'two thousand years and more ago, of God, an all-powerful God because God has to be all-powerful, taking millions, no, billions of years to form our planet and its life forms, could they? It'd have been beyond their comprehension. It's beyond the comprehension of most of us to this day. Six days work, rest on the seventh fits so much more conveniently with our current beliefs and established ways of life. Or,' Mark started, then stood gazing silently through the window at Lake Michigan for several seconds before continuing, 'did God only come much later?' But he shook his head no, and I did too.

He ceased his prowl and stood almost belligerently with his hands holding the back of a chair, eyes moving questioningly to mine. Again I smiled agreement and encouragement, and Mark re-opened his Bible to find another example, this one a verse in Revelation. He turned the Bible for me to read, finger pointing to verse fourteen. I read the part which explained--where she (the new Eve) is-- nourished for a time, and times, and half a time--. 'What period of time does "time, and times, and half a time," represent, sweetheart?' His arching eyebrows turned this into a question Mark expected me to answer.

'Haven't a clue, Hon,' I replied, shaking my head before continuing 'But it reinforces your argument, doesn't it, that extended periods of time could at best only be vaguely described by those who wrote about them way back.'

Mark started to look for another passage he had in mind in the modern Bible he'd brought, then suddenly and uncharacteristically snapped it shut without bothering to read and shrugged in resignation, saying with conviction, 'It's obvious, isn't it, languages have evolved along with humankind.'

I found no argument to counter his assertion.

We continued our discussion as we moved into the kitchen and helped ourselves to ham salad and rye crackers.

'I've been wondering recently,' Mark started after he'd swallowed a mouthful, 'what a computer-literate twenty-year old, starting with a blank screen and comparing the science of religion with that of evolution would come up with. Isn't most of what is critical to Christians' faith merely based on trust in beliefs without logical proof?'

Surprising myself I sprang quickly to Christianity's defence by countering, 'Look, Hon, let's face it, in most of recorded history, religion has given men and women universal direction, promises of forgiveness of sins and an afterlife. Those are huge inducements to believe, let's face it.'

Whose side was I on, I wondered. So did Mark.

'Hey, hang on, sweetheart,' Mark frowned at me in surprise, ' but isn't that direction, as you put it, innate now in humans anyway? It's right there in the frontal lobes of our brains from birth, surely? And tell me, what's the value of promises based on pure conjecture? What's the point in having life's anchor of hope set in sand?' Mark demanded, still frowning, leaning back and lifting his chair's two front legs off the floor as he clasped his hands behind his head, 'And we've just decided we've been taking the Bible too literally, haven't we?'

Indeed we had. My shoulders slumped.

I had certainly believed I spoke to God and my dead twin Brad at sixteen and seventeen. We, and our parents, have tithed all our working lives.

'Buying our way into Heaven,' Pop still says, only half jokingly.

But I believe, too, irrevocably now, that unless modern Christianity can reconcile with scientific discovery, its future is doomed, left in the dust of enlightenment passing it by.

Perhaps it's true to say that in the twenty-first century, belief in God lies between the bookends of science and evolution, and religion that fails to recognise that faces irrelevancy.

And does belief in God have much to do with religion anyway, I asked myself? There are, after all, different religions which believe in the same God.

Feeling back on track again, I remarked 'Scientists, after all, Hon, merely "discover" what's always been out there, but beyond understanding until humans learnt to read, write, and calculate, don't they?'

'Well put.' Mark agreed, giving me another smile and a thumbs-up. 'So what you're effectively saying, sweetheart, is that authentic scientific discovery could simply be divine revelation, right?'

'Right,' I agreed, before continuing, 'so, if God exists, He must have put it all in place from the very beginning, agreed?'

Nodding enthusiastically and sipping soda, Mark continued 'Why don't religious leaders and teachers cotton on to that, for heaven's sake, and wholeheartedly embrace the opportunity it presents them? Use it NOW, stop insisting that evolution is still a theory, except perhaps for so-called micro-evolution, and that the Genesis story is the real deal,' his urgency underlined by balling his fist and gently thumping the table for emphasis, ' before it's too late to gain moral and scientific high ground over some scientists who simply don't believe God created our planet and universe in the first place, and what's more are beavering away 24/7 to prove it. Christianity's credibility needs a major restoration job. No doubt about it.'

Shaking my head in frustration I answered, 'Because there's simply no incentive for anyone to want to change what has worked so well for hundreds of years, Hon. No, thousands, actually. Fear of Hell, the promise of redemption leading to a guaranteed place in Heaven. We know ancient Egyptians believed in an afterlife three thousand years before Christ, it was at the very heart of their religion, yet they had no sacred book, nor claims of divine truth.

'And just look how wealthy many churches became, individuals too, using this recipe! What about our own Crux? An annual turnover projected to be in excess of sixty-five million dollars over the next twelve months, selling franchises all over America and elsewhere, according to its website!

People really believe they can pay money to earn forgiveness for their sins and buy a ticket to Heaven!'

We sat in silence for a minute or two, pondering what we'd both been saying.

'How would Christ's second coming work in a situation like today's, I wonder?' Mark enquired speculatively on another tack, gently lowering his chair and unclasping his hands before continuing, 'I guess He'd read and write, be computer literate, drive a car?' He shrugged before continuing, 'Would He promote God's message on television, on radio, on line? Would Islamists place a fatwa on Him, like poor old Salman Rushdie had, or still does, for all I know?'

This interested me, what my man was saying, because an idea was buzzing around in my still somewhat confused head.

Back at our table silence reigned for a while as I sat with my head in my hands and eyes closed, deep in thought, Mark respecting my need for some silent introspection.

Could we possibly, I wondered seriously, Mark and Mary Lincoln, childless lawyers in the firm of Lincoln, Landless, and Partners, of Chicago, Illinois, somehow make a meaningful difference to the future of Christianity? Individuals certainly had in the past. Thousands of them. Apart from all kinds of different motives for doing so, but mostly serving their own selfish interests, men, women too, with no means of rapidly reaching distant audiences until recently, had contrived to alter the course of history in general, religion and Christianity in particular. Popes, Kings and Queens, clerics, soldiers, all had played their parts.

So it was possible, using modern information technology. But was it our problem, or much more to the point, our long-term future? Why shouldn't we just maintain the status quo, continue our lives of comfort as lawyers with a medium-sized fortune derived from the vagaries and frailties of human nature? Like Pastor Mick Warner, I couldn't help thinking, though his fortune was likely ten times ours, growing exponentially, it'd seem to me.

But I've right this very minute decided I simply have to know if God exists. And I want this to be proven by science or, at the very least, I thought, retracting a little because humans NEED God, to know that science cannot DISPROVE God's existence.

I believe there must be millions around the world who hope for the same. And now I feel a quickly growing belief and excitement that Mark and Mary Lincoln can indeed play a meaningful worldwide role in achieving this.

Pastor Warner's Christmas theme of beginnings was having a greater effect on at least two members of his flock than he could possibly have imagined, I thought, inwardly smiling somewhat ruefully.

My inheritance from Mom and Pop's steel business will be huge when they go, as will Mark's from his father, now battling motor neuron disease. We have no children. We'd start with strong financial foundations.

But we haven't yet followed some of our American dreams, I realised with a stab of dismay.

Like drawing the smell of Lakeshore's Harley-Davidson new leathers into our nostrils as we ride John Steinbeck's the Mother Road, Route 66, from the corner of Michigan Avenue and Jackson Boulevard, Mark on his Fat Hog, me on my Soft-Tailed Springer, to Ocean Avenue in Santa Monica. Eat at Dixie's Truck Stop, visit our namesake President's memorial in Springfield, take-in the panoramic view of Nevada, California, and Arizona from Sitgreaves Pass. Meander Los Angeles and Hollywood.

And we must continue looking after Mark's Pop until motor neuron disease inevitably throttles the agonised life out of him.

And how could God, I wondered for the umpteenth time, a caring, loving God, let one of His loved and loving good ones die like this?

Seems to me now the crux of our problem with the status quo is The Crux here in Chicago. Crux, "cross" in Latin, was making me cross. Both of us cross. It was Mick Warner who'd once told us Crux is also another name given to the Southern Cross, that constellation in southern night skies used for centuries by countless travellers to guide them safely over vast oceans and across harsh deserts.

My eyes were drawn inexorably back to our antique globe. From the birth-place of Christ, south across the equator to where scientists now believe lies the cradle of humankind, in Africa.

A fleeting thought crossed my mind. Our forebears came from Africa, white as we are. We'd just be making a journey back to our roots, if we took the new route in our lives the situation seemed to be demanding.

Mark was unusually quiet, deep in faraway reflection just as I'd been, I noticed with a glance.

Our thoughts so often coincide and coalesce, and this Christmas day was to prove no exception.

I spun the globe a full turn, drawing Mark's bright eyes and quick mind back to it and the present. It came to rest where it had started. Our eyes met in mutual understanding, then followed my forefinger tracing an imaginary journey west from Jerusalem to Cairo and the Nile in Egypt, south into Ethiopia, across the Horn of Africa, along The Great Rift Valley, southwards beyond the Tropic of Capricorn, finally coming to rest at Cape Town.

Matthew

Apart from their stunning good looks, Mark and Mary Lincoln made a huge impression on Hayley and me this evening, arriving on Harley-Davidsons they'd ridden all the way from Bethlehem via Cairo and Addis Ababa to Cape Town.

An American couple determined to start a new Christian sect in Africa they'll call *RELIGOLUTION,* Christianity believing God's existence will be revealed through a deeper and wider understanding of evolution, drawn to our Kenilworth restaurant by its name, Southern Cross.

Hayley later admitted to feeling weak at the knees when Mark first smiled at her, and Mary seemed to me to be about as far removed from the mother of Jesus image as I could imagine, more like a beautiful, blonde, vivacious wingless angel!

The Lincolns explained how they'd been on one of our Southern Cross Cape Wine Route Tours this afternoon, and received a recommendation (standard operating procedure by our multi-lingual tour guides) to try one of our restaurant franchises for dinner.

Their temporary B-and-B being situated in Kenilworth, they'd ended up at our flagship and first Southern Cross restaurant to meet us, its proprietors Matt and Hayley Draper.

Interestingly, Mary Lincoln told us as a teenager she believed she'd spoken to God and her dead twin brother in Heaven, but after a couple of years she had inexplicably lost the "connection", as she referred to it.

She was fascinated to hear I'd experienced what I also believed at the time was a similar ability, but which I later came to realise was my conscience talking to me, not God. I explained how I'd given my conscience the name Thomas, Doubting Thomas, years ago, and we have frequent conversations to this day!'

'Doubting Thomas? ' Mary exclaimed, laughing delightedly, 'Perhaps it was my conscience I was talking to then!'

In reply to their query about my own religious beliefs, I told the Lincolns I had an open mind, though generally veering towards the negative, on whether God exists. Thomas reminded me this wasn't REALLY how it was, so I was quick to add that I hoped *Religolution* would prove beyond doubt one way or the other, but preferably that God DOES exist.

'The thing I find hardest to understand is how believers give God all the credit for miraculous-seeming events, and even for such fleetingly mundane matters as success in the classroom or on the sports-field, yet never an iota of blame for anything that goes wrong, or becomes a disaster, despite that God made the world and everything in it.'

'But look here, folks, 'I NEED God,' I explained with simple conviction, 'probably everyone does, but only a God I can believe in unreservedly. I'd love nothing more than to have my faith fully restored. The Christianity into which I was brought up has lost all credibility for me, so its restoration project on which you're embarking interests me greatly. There are times when I call myself an agnostic, not knowing whether God exists or not, at others Deism attracts me, in that the acceptance of God is a supposition required by reason rather than revelation. So I'm with you all the way.'

'Count me in on it too!' Hayley added enthusiastically, touching my hand in solidarity.

Since we've been married, ten happy, fulfilling years and two kids down the line, Hayley and I've often discussed our beliefs (and doubts too) in great depth.

Our religious beliefs have converged somewhat over the decade. Mine were stronger than Hayley's to begin with, I went to junior and senior Anglican boarding schools, where we attended chapel seven days a week, and Divinity lessons in the classroom, while hers have become stronger from a base of practically zero.

Now we've come to believe the Bible is taken far too literally. We feel God needs a much more human face to be entirely credible, to bring Him closer to us, (assuming He's there), so that He's easily approachable.

Their interest then turned to Hayley, who in part explanation recounted the contents of a piece she'd written to me, tongue-in-cheek, soon after we'd met, to show how she believed we held the Bible in too much reverence.

"In the Beginning.........

Genesis tells us how God made us in His likeness, starting with Adam, the Hebrew word for person.

The human breeding programme mischievously started by Adam and Eve in the garden of Eden, perhaps after watching animals doing it, hit a serious God-planned snag with the flood, set in motion by God's deep regret at having made man and then woman, resulting in His determination to rid himself of them and their offspring, possibly because they were so interbred, and of every other creature on earth, though why He didn't appreciate His animals either nobody really knows.

Methuselah's grandson Noah, begat from Lamech, (who of course was begotten by Methuselah) and God had good rapport and a strong working relationship going, and so Noah was entrusted with building the Ark, and saving a core of God's creatures, including Noah and his wife, plus his family of three sons and their wives, to re-start the human race (talk about inbreeding!), after the rest had been wiped out by God flooding the earth.

At the end of Noah's epic voyage, the Captain cooked some of the surviving animals and fowls, earning God's blessing for the ensuing delicious smells and flavours of history's first recorded barbecue, and a covenant never to destroy all life on earth again. Never is a very long time!

Noah and his family restarted the human breeding programme with another of God's blessings and remarkably successful vigour. Their offspring begot and begat, by gad, going in unto their wives, and wifing their maids, as had their own forebears been begotten. Lot's two daughters got their father drunk and had an incestuous relationship with him.

Grandpa Methuselah had continued begetting for centuries before he finally passed on at the ripe old age of 969 before the flood, narrowly missing out on a tenth centenarian's congratulatory message from God.

Nevertheless, he is great- to-the-power-of-thousands grandfather to all of us here on earth now. Such a pity we never inherited his longevity gene!

God's propensity to destroy human life came to the fore again later when He flattened and burnt Sodom city, after a Dutch auction with Abraham, where God's opening bid of finding fifty righteous men in Sodom to save the city from destruction was finally lowered to a mere ten.

As there weren't even that number to be found there, the city was ruined, probably by earthquake, and burnt, likely by oil lamps falling over in the 'quake and setting light to escaping oil, gas, tar, or sulphur, all abundant under many Biblical cities. This sort of thing happens to this very day.'

Over an Irish coffee after their meal, Mark and Mary explained the main reason they'd come to Southern Cross was to establish how franchising worked in South Africa, by getting to discuss it with the owners of obviously successful ones, and here we were, doing just that.

Hayley and I were amazed to hear that not only was the Church of the Crux in Chicago selling franchises, but other American churches were too.

They'd realised with absolute clarity the only way they'd ever make a real, meaningful, enduring contribution to Christianity's ultimate survival was to explain that God himself put evolution into motion from the very beginning, it only being revealed once mankind learnt to read, write, and calculate.

They believe franchising to be the only viable option for the success of their crusade.

Hayley and I agree.

Our idea is to put them in touch with an organisation of which I'm a member, Y.E.A.S.T., Young Entrepreneurs Association Starting Trade, a networking group of over two hundred successful young business owners with a mission to help others reach for the stars.

As Y.E.A.S.T's bearded Chairman Chris Justes introduced Mark and Mary Lincoln to the assembled members, a buzz of incredulity greeted his announcement of their intentions to bring Christianity kicking and screaming into the twenty-first century, using franchising, and starting from a base in Cape Town.

Thanks to his legal background honed in countless courtroom battles, Mark's short induction application paper was presented concisely and convincingly.

He explained *RELIGOLUTION* was simply Christianity embracing scientific discovery of evolution as God's original blueprint, and belief that further revelations would confirm this.

A tolerant universal church respecting truth and searching for a common human ethic, where Christians and evolutionists would one day arrive at the same realisation and conclusion.

'Evolution and Christianity are not mutually exclusive. All life is related, surely a great basis for the existence of both God and evolution.

'During our journey here we visited Lake Malawi, scientifically renowned for having six hundred varieties of fish which have evolved from a single cyclid ancestor, and we saw with our own eyes the principle of divergence in operation, where the more they differed from each other, the better adapted they had become to using different parts of their environment.

'One of Charles Darwin's many critics of the time contemptuously remarked, "The world of nature, and The Reality of God." What he and others failed to understand was that by changing but a single short word of such pronouncements to read The World of Nature IS The Reality of God, they were much closer to the real truth!

'We hope and believe our creed will bring about a quiet religious revolution without rebellion, and a solution with solace to waverers on both sides of the line.'

By evolution, Mark left no doubt in the minds of those present, *Religolution* meant the "full monty", not what some reluctantly admit to, micro-evolution, supposedly to account for such differences as pigmentation in human populations around the world.

He further explained biologists now know every organism's DNA carries a record of its evolutionary past.

His statement that Allan Wilson's work redefines the meaning of "fossil" to include every human alive today opened the religiously myopic eyes of many Y.E.A.S.T. members to the inescapable reality of evolution.

Further research had been speeded up by concentrating on mitochondrial DNA, inherited only from the mother.

Additional work was being carried out by IBM and National Geographic with their Genographic project using Y-male chromosomes.

Evolutionists see with clarity how evolution is intrinsically linked to changed and still changing geography, how all life is related.

Comparing the embryos of a fruit fly and a human show remarkable similarity, and humans carry some of the same genes as butterflies or bananas.

Untrained human eyes see only the differences when comparing species, but there is underlying unity in diversification, as all living creatures share genes.

By sequencing genomes we can now read the new History of Life, showing a new historical narrative.

'Surely,' Mark said, and I watched faces in the audience intently, knowing what was coming, 'this is a great basis for believing in the existence of God.' As I'd expected, there were relieved smiles on many, encouraged by his obvious professional competence.

Mark explained how he and Mary had sold out of their law firm to partners to better concentrate their hearts, minds, and the rest of their lives to this crusade. Had spent eight months writing a " *Religolution's* Guide To Really Understanding The Bible," which was currently being printed in all major languages.

'We expect these will need to be regularly updated,' he assured them.

'In promoting *Religolution,* we promote the notion that the Bible's lessons, characters, and places reflect only what was then known of the limited world inhabited by the scribes of the time who wrote about them, with contents of Gospels selected for the Bible passed down through generations.

Genesis, for instance, explains that God's creation of our planet and all its living organisms took place over six eras or epochs, not six days. This, *Religolution* maintains, is simply allegorical.

'When God scattered Noah and his family's offspring abroad upon the face of all the earth from the city of Babel, it was not an event but an extended process.

'It is now common knowledge that our planet is billions of years old, but the flora and fauna on it much more recent. If one were to imagine condensing our planet's existence into a single 24-hour period, humankind would only have appeared during the last few seconds.'

Mark insisted that, for as long as Christianity continued to comprise faith-based religious flocks being fleeced of their spiritual and financial property in a frantic desire to buy their way into Heaven, by unscrupulous pastors peddling parables, Pharisees' fallacies and Philistines' fables, science would continue to erode that faith, and ultimately destroy it.

As it currently stands, he told the members, faith is no more than hope based on hearsay.

'There are some who will claim that's heresy, but not *Religolution,* based on scientific revelations it knows will ultimately distinguish fact from fiction. It seems to us, Bible literalists are at best misguided, at worst, deliberately misled.'

During the tea break Mark and Mary were inundated with queries and questions.

I overheard an ex-Zimbabwean white commercial farmer, one of thousands beaten up and unceremoniously booted off their farms years ago, question Mark on whether, if Africa was indeed the cradle of humankind as science seemed to indicate, the corollary of that suggested the rest of the world was colonised over millennia by Africans, so must have been in turn re-colonised by its own descendents going full circle, first black, then white, with DNA to prove it.

The ex-farmer, now a highly successful and respected Western Cape wine producer, smiled ruefully at Mark's affirmative reply.

In conclusion, Mark explained he and Mary had left America because much of its Christianity had become a vast conglomeration of power and money preaching dogma, and they believed it better for *Religolution* to quickly take root and grow rapidly in Africa, where multi-culturism hangs delicately in balance, and minds are more open to original thought, the separation of religious mystery from accurate history.

'Belief in God is not necessarily about religion, but if, and only if religion nurtures a belief in God that people feel completely comfortable with, can it be considered essential.'

Religolution's symbol and sign is a simple wooden cross depicting the Tree of Life, decorated with double helix DNA strands running from top to bottom and left to right, and Mary passed a rosewood example around the assembled gathering.

New developments in communications and information technology rapidly replacing the old and reaching even the furthest corners of the continent and the globe would help Mark and his wife expedite their crusade, he explained in conclusion.

Luke

One far corner of the earth's second-largest continent, known as The Horn of Africa, is an enduring world problem-area for reasons not associated with information technology, but where religion and poverty do play a significant role.

In particular, the blighted, war-torn, leaderless country of Somalia is fertile territory for exponential growth of dedicated terrorist cells.

Its modern-day pirates are amongst the most feared and therefore successful anywhere, paid multi-million dollar ransoms by helpless ship-owners and scared governments. Even ships hundreds of nautical miles from shore suffer their depredations.

In an attempt to counteract terrorist and pirate activities, several countries maintain permanent naval presences in the Indian Ocean's Somali Basin and the Gulf of Aden.

One such presence is the USS BISON, a command, control, and surveillance vessel of the United States Navy there on long-term station, under the command of Captain Luke Logan.

The ship's company are free to follow whatever political or religious persuasions they prefer as long as these are not pressed upon others, and all have 24/7 access to TV, internet, and worldwide radio.

Captain Logan and his three senior officers were carefully selected because of ability all possess over and above their remarkable naval proficiency, that of fluency in more than a dozen languages between them.

Logan and his Chief Engineer John Flanagan are also, in their limited spare time, budding volcanologists, and avid searchers for asteroids and meteorites using Bison's sophisticated equipment in the often clear Indian Ocean's night skies.

Both have a fascination tempered by real fear of the raw brute power and destructive ability of super volcanic eruptions and asteroid strikes on earth.

Daily they listen to chatter on the airwaves from two main sources, a multi-national scientific team based on the Indonesian Island of Sumatra, along the shores of Lake Toba, site of our planet's largest-ever known super volcanic eruption seventy-five thousand years ago, and an American team in the Mojave Desert watching space 24/7 for asteroids and meteorites as our planet revolves within it.

Bison's Captain particularly has a morbid interest in the end of the world as we know it, and from information filtering out of The Lake Toba Institute, Logan believes this could well be within his lifetime.

He worries that several virtually simultaneous strikes from a shower of extremely large asteroids could set off a world-wide chain reaction of earthquakes, volcanic eruptions, and tsunamis with apocalyptic consequences.

Rapidly melting ice-caps, glaciers, and snow had already raised and continued to raise sea levels world wide, exacerbating the likely effects of tsunamis and storm surges on susceptible coastal cities, towns, villages, and crop land.

In addition, this rise in sea levels could be significantly altering forces acting upon movements of all tectonic plates.

These views are not contradicted by science, as far as he's aware.

During really bad and depressing moments, the Bison's skipper also has further melancholy thoughts on his mind, such as rapid polar shift and its possible consequences, and the Mayan Calendar apparently ending soon, thereby gaining considerable worldwide notoriety as the Mayan Prophecy, depicting the end of our planet as we know it in our lifetimes.

The Armageddon promised in the Bible's New Testament, the Captain surmises.

But he now knows, deep under the present Lake Toba's placid surface, filling one of the world's largest known volcanic craters, scientific measurements indicate the existence of vast layer upon layer of magma building once again, only this time in even greater quantities than before.

And there seems no reason not to suppose this applies to many other scattered volcanic sites too.

Scientists have calculated, from samples found around the world, that the first Toba super eruption, boosted by almost three thousand cubic kilometres of magma, spewed billions of tons of rock, ash, and sulphur dioxide into the atmosphere, turning into sulphuric acid as it spread around the globe, destroying all life in its path.

In addition, it quickly and comprehensively changed the earth's climate, causing an ice-age lasting about a thousand years.

Current scientific projections put present magma build-up at five thousand cubic kilometres, already almost double the previous amount.

Luke Logan's religious beliefs are a confused jumble of hopes and fears, none more real than the fear of violence caused by 'an act of God.'

Constantly searching for solace from his fears, Luke Logan is hoping and searching for religious relief, but with diminishing conviction he'll ever find it.

His interest is piqued, however, on accessing *RELIGOLUTION*'s website.

"Christianity embracing scientific discovery as God's original work." This is right up his street, and the Captain joins its internet newsgroup.

To Mark and Mary he explains his fears and his reasoning behind them, and is somewhat mollified to learn *Religolution* is of the opinion that what scientists currently confidently predict will happen sooner or later is really no different to the Bible's prophecies in Revelations, using *Religolution's* Guide To Really Understanding The Bible.

'And if you think Lake Toba is going to be big, then I suggest you get to know what's going on under Yellowstone National Park, Captain Luke Logan,' was a suggestion made by a recent South African visitor to Yellowstone in a letter to *Religolution's* newsgroup.

Leila

Out of Bison's sight over the distant western horizon lies the virtually ruined Somali capital of Mogadishu, daily ravaged by callous warlords fighting brutally amongst themselves and against United Nations peacekeepers for control over small areas of seemingly worthless territory.

An apparent oasis on the periphery of this on-going chaos is the rapidly growing orphanage run by Leila bint Hammadi, an exotically beautiful and sensuous twenty-nine year old citizen of Saudi Arabia.

She has five female helpers, carefully selected citizens of five nuclear powers, America, Russia, Britain, Pakistan, and India. All have undergone training by Al Qaeda on the high mountains in the remote border region between Pakistan and Afghanistan.

Leila is painstakingly working on her assignment, ordered by Osama bin Laden himself, to jolt the nuclear powers into destroying one another by the simple ruse of making each of the governments concerned believe they're about to be attacked by one or more of the others.

This involves nothing more subtle than Leila's five operatives travelling under their own names, using their own passports, back to their countries of birth, and feeding news media there simultaneously with a diabolically clever story.

Leila and her dedicated team are working towards being ready when the President of the United States will be assassinated by a personal security guard.

Every three months, though not simultaneously, Leila's operatives openly travel to their own countries and successfully raise funds for their ever-growing orphanage, becoming widely known and well respected in the process for their dedicated service to abandoned orphans in arguably the world's most dangerous city. Christian churches are a good source of funds, and *Religolution* is approached for its help too.

It's not only potential funding though which interests Leila bint Hammadi about *Religolution*. Some sixth sense warns this new Christian sect may become a worldwide threat to Islam itself, and to prevent that she would proudly sacrifice her life and those of her co-workers.

She decides she'll visit what she sees as the viper of *Religolution* in its Cape Town nest.

Matthew

With respect to my darling wife Hayley, Leila bint Hammadi is the most sensually attractive woman I've ever seen, not least because of an aura of suppressed and dangerous fervour sparking her enormous, flashing, gem-black eyes under a fringe of shining straight hair the same colour.

Hayley, Mark, and Mary can hardly keep their eyes off her either.

She explained she'd studied business practice at Harvard, ' Right in the heart of Islam's great enemy,' she'd informed us in perfect English, with no hint of American accent and an enigmatic smile.

At her request, here are Hayley and I taking Leila for a tour around the Cape Flats, an area best known to the outside world for its dire poverty and horrendous crime rate, where the only running water is through roofs when it rains.

She's determined to understand how we Capetonians are going about changing the perceptions of those left in the dust of our government's so-called Black Economic Empowerment, or BEE, passing them by, though her arrival in the Mother City was primarily to discuss *Religolution* franchises in Mogadishu with Mark and Mary, she's told them, but it sounds fishy to us.

Actually, it was Thomas who issued that warning.

Mark and Mary, in partnership with Hayley and I, have put into practice alongside *Religolution* the notion that following simple, sound business principles with our help will further enhance poverty-stricken lives, and remove them from perpetual squalor and battles with the law, something so far religion seems unable to do on its own.

Our driver Sarel, his apparently toothless yellowy-brown face punished by excess and puckered like an over-ripe granadilla, guides us to his hand-painted blue and yellow ramshackle minibus of barely recognisable make and unknown vintage.

Obviously suffering terminal metal fatigue, it finally clatters into life, enveloping seven or eight cheering brown-skinned urchins pushing it in oily blue smoke.

'Sarel and his mini-bus,' I explain to Leila as we settle tentatively onto the bone-hard hand-made seats listing alarmingly, and watching her reaction with interest from the corners of our eyes, 'are a small but important part of the wider process we're going to experience in the next three hours or so.'

We lurch forth in a metallic convulsion.

'Just like Mogadishu!' Leila informs us, with a stunning smile of happy nostalgia that makes me wonder why she's not yet married an obscenely wealthy sheik. Too hot to handle, is my preliminary finding. Men in the Middle East would kill just to catch a glimpse of her, it wouldn't surprise me.

Our erratic journey along sandy tracks is accompanied wherever we go by wide smiles and cheerful waves that'd delight visiting royalty.

My sideways glances confirm a growing conviction that this carer of some of the world's most traumatised orphans is finding this experience uplifting. Leila frequently requests me to ask Sarel to stop.

'Just look at them, I need to touch them. Please!' At each group of small kids playing noisily on non-existent pavements, Leila climbs out after wrestling her door open, sinks to her knees on the warm dry sand, and holds her arms out to them. They come as if drawn by an irresistible, invisible force.

Once or twice I notice Hayley's eyes moistening.

Finally we grind to a juddering halt outside what appears at first glance to be simply a rather large shack, topped with rusty corrugated iron roofing, and walls of cardboard boxes belatedly advertising their erstwhile contents belying its true purpose.

This is, in fact, one of our franchises, a Southern Cross restaurant, first of many we've established in the poorest shack-strewn suburbs where there are dozens now, each one close to a *Religolution* facility.

TwentyWhen?

Spectacularly overweight owner-manager and Sarel's cousin Mama Graca, named after Nelson Mandela's wife's first visit, showed her Arab visitor around her spotless dining-room and kitchen, proud smile dimpling several chins.

Asked by Leila about the sort of food she offered, Mama Graca explained in a roundabout way, rolling words around her mouth like a large boiled sweet, 'We DON"T do what many restaurants do, have swarms of scurrying waiters serving stingy scalded stir-fries of scallops, scad, and scampi, or sugary stuffed strudels on stylish silver salvers, or sukiyaki and sushi served at syzygy with sake.'

Leila threw back her head, clapping and laughing delightedly. 'And what is this word syzygy, Mama Graca?' she giggled.

'You don't know syzygy, madame?' Pointing to me and with a sideways glance, Mama Graca passed the buck. 'Ask Meneer Draper here. He is the one who taught me this saying when he helped me and my family start our restaurant!' she ended triumphantly, arms akimbo over her ample bosom.

Suppressing a smile, I obliged by replying 'Syzygy means a conjunction of the sun and moon, Leila. It's a bit of nonsense really, but sort of shows what Southern Cross Restaurants are all about, simplicity in every aspect. Best quality fresh seasonal ingredients, cooked with care and served with flare, promoting and showcasing local food styles in friendly environments.

'This restaurant and its twin *Religolution* facility--not a church in the generally accepted sense of the word, it's more of an information centre--outsource to their surrounding community. Vegetable growers, fishermen, horse and cart operators who carry produce and do township tours, bands which play music for the believers and the eaters, maintenance crews, builders, carpenters, plumbers, tour bus operators, and minibus drivers such as our Sarel.

'In this way the whole community stands to participate and benefit, lifting themselves out of crime and poverty, to use a cliché, by their own bootstraps.'

'But with absolutely vital initial input from you and Hayley, Mark and Mary, including start-up finance.' Leila added, summing up what had already become obvious to her.

Beautiful AND sharp, is Leila bint Hammadi!

'Oh yes.' I replied, as Mama Graca served us her wonderful Malay fish curry, cunningly spiced and seasoned with ingredients she refuses to divulge even to me or Hayley, laughing uproariously and shaking her head whenever we press her, explaining it's a secret passed on by her grandmother's mother, 'but with a signed loan agreement,' I continued. 'We believe this is the only basis for enduring advancement, ownership.

'And Mama Graca's Southern Cross restaurant repaid its loan easily within its first year of operation. So did all other business units associated with it and its twin *Religolution* franchise too.

Mama Graca smiled proudly at this compliment.

Carrying on, I explained 'Of course, once that happened, it was easy to get other groups to follow in their footsteps, and to date we've set-up thirty-seven in the Cape Town metropolitan area, with only one of them defaulting.

'But now we're taking it another step further, so that these folk realise they can start to dream, really dream that there is no end to what they can achieve and to finally believe, too.

'How many groups are operating countrywide, then?'

'Two hundred and seventy-four now, with more than half that number again in the pipeline. By the end of our third year we'll have more than five hundred up and running. In conjunction, the Southern Cross and *Religolution* franchises have done better than we'd hoped in our wildest early dreams. Each sells the other, you see.'

'Perhaps you could do something similar in Mogadishu?' Hayley enquired helpfully.

As Leila heard that, though, a veil seemed to slide over her eyes, which she cast disconsolately down at the ground before replying quietly, 'I am a Muslim, and a woman. In my adopted country I cannot run a business, but perhaps some of my co-workers could.'

After enjoying our superb lunch, which brought lavish praise from all three of us for Mama Graca, we decided to press on for Leila to experience other elements of our grand plan in operation.

Our departure was delayed several minutes, however, while an impromptu game of street soccer involving Sarel, wheezing like a leaking concertina, and nine or ten teenagers, several of them his nephews, came to a raucus end as our driver's surprising ball skills saw him scoring the winning goal with a clever back-heel.

The soccer players finally got us going again, pushing and coaxing Sarel's vehicle back into reluctant action, but not before the rear-view mirror had given up its tenuous grip on the cracked windscreen and clattered to the floor, and the spare wheel been run over as it fell from its bay.

Unfazed, Sarel fished out a tube of SuperGlue from his pocket and restored the mirror to its rightful place while his nephews wrestled the spare wheel back where it belonged.

'My new 12-seater Toyota Minibus will be ready for me next week, Mr Draper, the delay was caused by the colour I wanted, yellow and purple,' Sarel proudly informed us, which didn't surprise Cassie and I, but impressed Leila, who leant forward and patted his thin shoulder, saying ' 'Congratulations, Sarel.'

Leila watched as I paid Sarel for the journey, just as I'd done for Mama Graca's meal, clapping silently so's I could see.

The last leg of our township tour entailed a short journey in a colourful Cape cart pulled by a single big bay horse, during which a trifling incident en-route reminded me of a story my English grandfather used to tell, and which I repeated to Leila now.

In his young days as a mounted policeman in London, he'd been assigned to ride security alongside the royal carriage carrying King George the Sixth, Queen Elizabeth, and the two princesses.

Trotting down the Mall, he'd found himself within arm's length of the future young Queen. Suddenly, Grandpa's horse farted loudly. Embarrassed, he leant towards Princess Elizabeth and out of the corner of his mouth said just loud enough for her to hear, 'Pardon, Ma'am.'

Startled, the Princess replied loud enough for them all to hear, 'Oh, I thought it was the horse.'

This little tale brought but a shy smile from Leila, who was, however, at the end of our tour lavish in her praise of what Hayley and I, Mary and Mark had achieved in such a short time.

She returned to her Kenilworth hotel with a promise to come back for lunch the next day at our Kenilworth restaurant for a final chat before her departure for Mogadishu via Nairobi.

Leila

Leila bint Hammadi was in a quandary, an unusual state for her sharp, perceptive, scheming mind, pacing her hotel room back and forth, glancing distractedly each circuit at the imposing Table Mountain massif through her large picture window.

She'd come to Cape Town ready and able to eliminate the vipers who'd started *Religolution* in their nest, but was it already too late, she wondered?

Reluctantly admiring what the couples had already spectacularly achieved in uplifting the lives of hundreds of thousands of underprivileged people, and balancing that against what effect it could have on Islam itself was really no contest in the greater scheme of things.

Her resolve and heart hardened, as indestructible as that mountain. Their structures were not yet fully self-perpetuating, Leila decided, and once the roots of this particular tree were cut--the sooner the better--its branches and leaves would wither and die too.

They would never know. Neither would the South African Police Services. She would use the tiny 'skin freshener' spray she always kept within easy reach for their termination.

Arriving at Southern Cross for lunch at one, Leila was surprised and highly frustrated to learn from Hayley and Mary their husbands had left at short notice on the early-morning shuttle for an urgent meeting in Johannesburg, later.

She'd have to delay her assassinations and departure from Cape Town at least until then, meanwhile informing her five assistants in Mogadishu of her delayed return.

Back in her Kenilworth hotel suite she sent an Arabic text message to them. This message was received simultaneously in the orphanage outside Mogadishu, and aboard U.S.S. Bison, where all Arabic messages containing any one of several hundred words were for the immediate attention of Captain Luke Logan himself, the ship's Arabic specialist.

Luke

Appended to this text were precise locations of sender and receiver, in Cape Town and Mogadishu.

As Logan happened to be on *Religolution's* website at the time, and knew of Leila bint Hammadi's visit to *Religolution's* heaquarters, immediately he'd translated it he knew it required his urgent attention and appropriate reaction. It also informed him of another fanatical terrorist cell in Mogadishu to add to his growing list.

"solution delayed" told him, as surely as if the message had been directed to him personally, that *Religolution* was to be attacked and destroyed, and the "delay" indicated might be of extremely short duration.

Captain Logan did something way outside his terms of reference, he personally contacted *Religolution's* Cape Town head office, where after a short delay he spoke to Hayley Draper, and by the end of a two-minute telephone conversation Hayley knew Leila was planning a deadly strike on *Religolution's* founders and promoters, no doubt soon after Mark and Matt's return.

Matthew

Mark and I arrived at the world's deepest worked-out gold mine within twenty-five kilometres of Johannesburg city centre by seven-thirty this morning.

Here, Mark and I, in conjunction with most of Y.E.A.S.T"'s members and several of the world's most distinguished space-travel scientists, have established a secret underground space-travel laboratory and production facility, unknown to the world at large, but proudly sanctioned by the inner coterie of the South African Government, and it's to an urgent meeting of this eminent group that Mark Lincoln and I've been summoned for reasons as yet unknown.

We all of us here share a belief the world could end in our lifetimes, and we feel a responsibility to humankind to do what we can to extend its existence on earth if what appears likely to happen does, though of course we realise God will step in somehow----if He's there (or right here!) and can.

There'll no doubt be those who point fingers and say 'See, *Religolution* doesn't believe in God and His plans for us either.' Well, the straight answer is we're still waiting for science to prove that God exists, or that there's no proof He doesn't, and we've never made any secret of that.

There's a strong and almost palpable element of self-preservation amongst us. I guess it's just basic human instinct to survive as long as we can in any way we can, isn't it?

To this end we're all totally committed to the success of our group's Armageddon Regeneration Key project, otherwise known as ARK-2.

Ark Spaceplanes are designed for autopilot launch from underground pads via vertical shafts, orbital link-up, separation, and landing, at the discretion and direction of the Flight Manager, and today we're going to see the first Arks ready for testing in space, we've just been informed, thus accounting for the secrecy and urgency of our unexpected summons.

In addition, we're all to undergo our first in-house training sessions as Flight Managers, not to be confused with pilots. Arks fly themselves. We simply tell them when we want our journeys to start and where they'll end.

I must say I was almost stunned by the powerful and elegant beauty of Ark's clean lines, the spaceship somehow smaller than I'd imagined, though with a much roomier interior than seemed possible from the outside.

Like everything associated with the ARK project, we're in awe of its simplicity as far as its Flight Manager's controls are concerned. A green 'READY FOR TAKEOFF" button pressed after entering a password, a large screen showing continuous moving real-time images of our planet, including the side hidden from view at any point in orbit, with adjustable magnification enabling us to read the maker's name on a golf ball in play on earth. Simply stunning! And lastly a 'LAND AT' button pressed when an adjustable moving red dot is placed on the desired position on the map of the earth's surface.

After spending one of the most fascinating hours of our lives in the Ark simulator, from where we watched a hurricane building off the coast of Haiti, and work-in-progress on Dubai's offshore development The World, we joined others in the Flight Origination Centre where we were addressed by the facility's Operations Director.

To a huge collective gasp of amazement he announced, his features barely able to conceal a smile of tremendous pride and pleasure, 'In thirty minutes, Arks Zero One AND Zero Two will be launched for a twenty-four hour test flight. This will be the first the world--apart from the South African Government of course--will know of our programme. It can no longer be kept secret, obviously, as led by the Americans, the world's surveillance facilities will pick up the launch, follow both spaceplanes' flight paths, witness them docking in orbit, separating, and returning to earth at O.R. Tambo International.

'Of course,' he continued when the shouting, hugging, clapping, and air-punching had died down, 'we can expect the world's media to be here in full force within hours, but we have made provision for our publicity agents to handle that aspect.'

Pointing, the Operations Director said, 'May I suggest we all follow the green route back to the surface and watch!'

There was a spontaneous surge to lead the way, like boarding-school boys let out for the beginning of long summer holidays.

Thomas, my ever Doubting Thomas, asked an interesting question to which I certainly had no immediate answer.

Were we, Southern Cross Franchises and *Religolution,* never mind all the other Y.E.A.S.T. members, ready for the phenomenal world-wide clamour of interest in our work on space travel, and demand for all our other diverse services too, after these flights using new-to-the-scientific-world technology in a successful launch, orbital docking, and safe landing? Obviously the short answer is NO! But what a challenge, I replied.

Perhaps the launch as we witnessed it from above ground was not quite as spectacular as those of America's Challenger series, because the Arks shot straight out and up from separate underground launch pads, one immediately after the other, already travelling at five hundred kilometres per hour, we were informed by flight control. But the sound and vibration as they rapidly climbed before disappearing from sight almost directly above us is likely to remain etched in our memories for ever.

As docking was scheduled for six hours after launch, Mark and I decided, as did most of the rest of Y.E.A.S.T's members, though not the boffins, to follow proceedings from television in our own homes with our families and friends, and duly caught the bus back to O.R.Tambo, from where we took the first available flight back to Cape Town.

Twenty minutes into the flight, our Captain informed passengers and crew of what he termed 'incredible news of the successful launch and flight into orbit simultaneously of two manned spaceplanes, developed and manufactured in South Africa, from a site apparently close to Johannesburg.'

Before Mark and I disembarked at Cape Town International, Thomas asked me another awkward question, one which somewhat spoiled our triumphal return, enquiring what we'd do if we happened to be on an ARK when the world was covered in volcanic ash, there was no life left, and so nowhere to land when water and food on board ran out.

Luckily I don't always feel the need to answer Doubter immediately.

Our arrival back at our joint office complex in Kenilworth near Cape Town was greeted with happy surprise at our early return, and congratulations from Hayley and Mary on the overwhelming success of the Y.E.A.S.T. initiative, immediately tempered, though, by deep concern for our safety from possible imminent fatal attack from Al-Qaeda operative Leila bint Hammadi herself, about which we heard with mounting trepidation.

'Told you,' Doubting Thomas reminded me, ' her claim to be in Cape Town for appraisal of *Relogolution* franchises sounded fishy.'

Fishy, from what Hayley told me of her phone conversation with Captain Luke Logan, was putting it mildly. Leila was extremely fanatical, deadly, and determined, and the Captain's suggestion was to tell her we knew the real reasons for her being in Cape Town, and whilst watching her like hawks, physically escort her to the airport departure gate and make sure we personally watched her onto her flight, followed by its ascent into clear summer skies in a northerly direction.

Logan had also commented that bint Hammadi's work as a carer of traumatised orphans, though laudable in itself, was nevertheless a clever front for something diabolical.

'To think we spent a whole day with an Al-Qaeda assassin!' Hayley said, shuddering, appalled, holding her cheeks with both hands, eyes wider than I've ever seen them as she looked first at me, then in turn at the others.

Thinking back on it myself now, I realised I'd probably have soiled my jeans if I'd had the barest inkling of what Leila had planned to do, to me and the rest of us involved in *Religolution*.

I imagined those sparking black eyes boring into mine as she silently slid a sharp knife into my heart, and experienced a real and pressing desire to visit the bathroom immediately, feeling as weak as Samson must've after his haircut.

Of course every available television news channel was dedicated to telling the world everything they were being fed by ARK PROJECT

INFORMATION, and other information erroneously guessed-at by so-called space specialists, unaware until the spaceships were actually orbiting of their existence, and nothing whatever of their *raison d'etre*.

Leila

Still in her hotel room, Leila bint Hammadi was glued to television news channels too, unaware that two of her four quarries were already back in Cape Town, hours sooner than originally anticipated.

Her quick mind was working at a frantic pace. She felt growing certainty that both the Draper and Lincoln families were somehow intimately involved with the picture developing, literally minute-by-minute, and the reasons being given for the Armageddon Regeneration Key project, ARK-2.

And she'd detected some sense of not being told the truth by Cassie and Mary upon her arrival for lunch earlier.

It was taking coincidence too far to believe Matt and Mark had gone to Johannesburg unexpectedly at short notice on the very day this momentous development occurred, and not have played a significant role in its planning and financing.

But did this development in any way change her perception of what should be done, she demanded of herself?

Was this so-called ARK-2 useful in any conceivable shape or form to the ultimate survival of Islam, unlikely as that seemed now?

Leila watched fascinated as the two spaceplanes locked smoothly together.

Five minutes later, after watching the same images the orbiting crews were, a Twenyt20 cricket match at Sahara Newlands Cricket Ground, literally only a short distance from where Leila sat now, (she could hear the crowd reactions and applause through her open window), the two spacecraft, proudly displaying along their sides the South African flag, *Religolution's* cross with its double helix DNA strands of decoration, Southern Cross and other companies' logos, and the Y.E.A.S.T. emblem, smoothly undocked but remained in formation. What she saw confirmed her diagnosis of the Draper/Lincoln involvement.

Leila bint Hammadi found herself in another quandary. Armageddon Regeneration Key? ARK-2? What an extraordinary concept! As sure as night followed day, when Allah decided the world would end Allah would end it if that was Allah's intention, and if Allah decided mankind required regeneration, Allah would organise that too.

And didn't the mere fact this so-called Ark-2 existed show beyond any reasonable doubt *Religolution* was merely a money-making scam, nothing to do with true belief even in Christianity's God? Yes, the four of them would have to die, Leila decided, feeling a surge of sublime power coursing through her.

Matthew

The adrenaline coursing through my veins at the prospect of possible imminent death made me feel weak at the knees, yet grimly determined to carry out Luke Logan's exhortation to get this Arab killer out of our lives and South Africa.

Mark, having dealt with murderers in courts of law, defended and prosecuted them, looked into their eyes and perhaps even into the depths of their souls, would, I knew, be best to organise this illegal eviction.

He would lead, the three of us would follow.

Thomas, with his usual excruciating timing, said he knew I wasn't a coward at heart, just preferred to watch certain things happen rather than make them happen. I chose once more to keep my council for the time being.

We held a quick, urgent meeting, Mark and Mary, Hayley and I, and unanimously agreed to follow Captain Luke Logan's urgings to the letter.

We bought an internet ticket for our potential assassin on the next flight out of Cape Town leaving in less than ninety minutes, and five minutes later, thanks to the Hotel Manager being a personal friend of Haylie's and mine, we swarmed into Leila's bedroom, led by Mark. Determined to maintain our element of surprise, we closely watched her every move.

Apart from Mark's brusque 'We know your real objective. Your taxi to the airport is already waiting downstairs,' nobody spoke, our actions speaking louder than any words, Leila immediately aware her game was up.

Her bag was in any case already packed, our nearly-assassin ready for a rapid getaway under her own terms. With the tables turned, Mark, using his six feet two inch height, laser eyes, and contemptuous court prosecutor's manner to maintain our advantage, in what seemed a trice had Leila carrying her own bag down to and inside a waiting taxi.

This was as smart a sting as any I've ever watched on T.V., I thought proudly, as I made a hasty arrangement at reception to pay her bill a couple of hours later.

The taxi driver's eyes lit up at the sight of the payment in advance Mark thrust at him, and we had to really hurry along to keep up with him and his passenger on the fifteen-minute dash to the airport.

As the assassin disembarked, Mark thrust her ticket into her hand at arm's length, and peremptorily indicated the DEPARTURES sign.

If the look in Leila's eyes was anything to go by, because I momentarily looked into them and instantly wished I hadn't, she would do the business for which she'd come regardless, in the not-too-distant future.

The sense of relief as we watched the Boeing 737 departing Cape Town was tangible, and we happily celebrated our reprieve from death with a champagne gargle back at the restaurant. The first bottle didn't really do the business, in fact I've passed urine stronger than that, so we had another to belatedly toast the stunning ongoing success of ARK-2.

That evening, Hayley and I, with our kids Brett and Tamsin, by now fully acquainted with their parents' involvement in ARK-2 and inordinately proud of it, began discussing our options if in our lifetimes the need arose for us to get away from an Armageddon-type scenario.

Now I haven't mentioned this to you before, because it's only now become relevant to what I'm telling you.

My father, who was a senior officer in the South African Navy during the Second World War, was deeply involved (no pun intended!) in a government scheme to hide five hundred well-armed and provisioned elite troops deep underground.

This was to mitigate the effects of a possible nuclear attack on Cape Town by maintaining a core of men safe to help survivors in the event such an attack occurred.

With the benefit of hindsight, this was an inordinately hair-brained solution to a most unlikely event. Be that as it may, much frantic burrowing had occurred deep inside a hillside not far from Simonstown Naval Dockyard, out of sight of prying eyes.

What became an embarrassment at war's end was sold for a song to the highest bidder of a hurriedly convened, non-advertised auction, and the Draper family of Kenilworth became the warren's somewhat less-than-proud owners.

And right now we were considering whether it might be an Armageddon option, rather than floating in space in an ARK.

'Oh Dad, Mom, I want to watch Armageddon happening, not be hiding underground where we can't see and know what's happening on our planet!' Brett exclaimed, with unexpected passion from our twelve-year old.

I could feel Thomas getting ready to put his oar in at my reply, or more correctly, at my imminent equivocation.

'We have to be aware, chaps, (the calm voice of reason here) that we'll probably have some roster plan in action for the ARKS, don't forget there'll only be about ten of them altogether.'

'Dad!' our argumentative ten-and-half-year old daughter Tamsin exclaimed vehemently, continuing with a lisp enhanced by several gaps in her teeth and a formidable set of braces, ' thath not twoo, Daddy, I thaw on Tv thouthandth wiw be fwying by Kwithmith, it theemth the whole world waa' to fwy in one.'

The Draper second team had certainly laid their cards right-side-up on the table, and what was Hayley's answer going to be, I wondered, with unusual uncertainty. We three looked across at her in anticipation.

Doubter muttered something to the effect that I'd look foolish if my wife sided with our offspring. I retorted sharply that wherever the majority decided to go, he, Thomas, had no option but to follow, and to do me a favour and shud-uppa-your-face.

But Thomas wouldn't give up, saying my face-saving idea of a vote qualified by the fact our kids are under eighteen I was beginning to consider is rubbish, and having started this decision-making process on equal terms, there was no going back on it.

I suppose by now you the reader will know where I'd rather be--in the Simonstown burrow. Thomas muttered coward, but I'm just ignoring it.

One possible reason for NOT going into the burrow though, for what could become--probably would become--an extended sojourn, is the thought of Thomas's constant carping criticism in such a confining space, the little jerk.

Surely Hayley would prefer the burrow option too?

But I most certainly do want to spend some time in space before there's any sign of Asteroid strikes, or a super volcano starts its deadly spewing.

My level-headed wife and mother of our children, with the wisdom of Solomon, said that as we spoke, we didn't actually currently even have an option.

The Simonstown underground bunker, she noted, would take months to be made ready for extended occupation, and ARK-2 was still undergoing extensive and extended testing, and therefore the only sensible plan was to get the bunker ready in the interim, by which time ARK-2 testing might be over, and we could make up our minds then.

I was really quite annoyed with myself for not thinking of that first. As no-one came up with any counter proposals, our discussion ended rather lamely, for which I was grateful.

'Whew!' I exhaled, 'I declare this meeting closed.'

Lucky! murmured Doubter.

Work on what we came to refer to as Bolters' Burrow continued intermittently between pressures of work on all franchise fronts, but our family gradually built a consensus of pride in what we were achieving there, and I thought once or twice I detected a smidgen of envy in Mary and Mark when they were invited to assess our project's suitability for purpose.

Mary

Mark and I are spending much of our time away from Cape Town--it really is both 'The Fairest Cape' and 'The Cape of Storms' in different seasons--keeping abreast of developments in the scientific world which we believe are pertinent to *Religolution*.

And this covers both evidence of potentially catastrophic events affecting our planet, and advances in science's understanding of genetics, and therefore of evolution.

We've been surprised, but of course delighted, at how far and wide the reason for and message of *Religolution* has spread, and is still continuing to spread at an ever-increasing pace, moving way beyond Africa.

Of course it's not all been plain sailing. Far, far from it. The episode involving our near-death experience with Leila bint Hammadi has been by miles the scariest so far for sure, but we've received death threats from places as far apart as Wellington, Wichita, and Ouagadougou.

Mark is certain, and I'm inclined to agree with him now, that it's not so much our creed that is unacceptable to certain pastors and clerics, but its effect on their bottom lines, with congregations demanding answers to awkward questions about some of their teachings, something not experienced for decades, centuries even.

Supporting this contention is what Mark found on his most recent return to our former home in Chicago, which we have kept on in anticipation of one day using it as a base for our American arm of *Religolution*, when we judge that time is ripe.

Visiting incognito, Mark attended morning service one Sunday at The New Timber Bay Community Church of The Crux again, wondering if he'd find it any easier to take now than it'd been for us on its Christmas opening, which had so significantly changed our lives, and those of millions more, it must be said.

Far from it.

Mick Warner had become a Televangelist in the intervening years, one of the most popular in the nation, and in many other Christian parts of our planet where his messages were broadcast daily. He'd specifically trashed *Religolution* as being 'The Devil's divisive device to destroy Christianity,' as a slightly amused Mark had sat and passively listened.

'Hon, not much change there,' Mark had remarked laconically on his return to Cape Town.

Together we sat and read the latest batch of e-mails, pretty representative of those we've been receiving all along, really. We continue to ignore the rude and threatening ones, whilst replying to those who feel enlightened and enriched.

Here's a cross-section of them:

Infidels, may thousands of camels shit on your lawns.

Osama.

May you rot in eternal hell and damnation.

I.C.Redd.

You're on a one-way ticket to Hell, and so are your followers.
Good riddance.
P.S. I hope you all suffer a plague getting there.

You have given a new lease to my life. Belief and Hope have returned Big Time.

Broken Cane, Headmaster,
Hiawatha High School U.S.A.

Because we learnt about the formation of our planet and the evolution of its life forms in Zambia before we were introduced to Christianity here, we did not believe in God. Thanks to Religolution, now we do. We cannot possibly praise you enough.

Pennysave and Godwills Gwatidzo. Oxford, England.

You have finally shed bright light on what seemed an insoluble riddle. Long live God the Father, God the Son, God the Holy Ghost.

Pastor Turner Page. New Zealand.

During Islam's Empire of Reason, Islamist scholars were searching for truth about science and geography, and building devices to reliably measure them, while you Europeans still slumbered in The Dark Ages.

What right has your upstart organisation got to believe it can change belief?

Proud Saudi Citizen and True Believer.

I don't know how to handle Religolution in my job. I wholeheartedly embrace its creed, but my School Board (and others before this one), precludes meaningful discussion on the evolution of mankind. You have put me in a real quandary.

Do I abandon my calling, or continue as though nothing has changed? Is that immoral?

Guthro Guthrie III, Pennsylvania.

Before Mark and I embarked on our first space odyssey we sounded out several recent astronauts, and found those who unreservedly believed in God before space flight became certain He was close to them in space, and still there back on earth when they returned to it, whilst the disbelievers became equally convinced of the opposite.

Not much help there.

Our own experiences initially produced utter awe at the boundless enormity of our vast universe, the apparent inconsequentiality of our puny blue planet earth within it surrounded by its thin film of air, and a deafening sound of silence within what we now both understand is the reason for being called Deep Time.

'There's so much more to all this than one can possibly imagine from earth,' was my husband's first comment as he surveyed the slowly cart-wheeling scene in wonderment, and the Ark's engines closed down after we swung seamlessly into earth orbit.

As for me, I could find no words to adequately express either what I saw, or thought.

Certainly God was there somewhere in the turmoil of my mind, but in precisely what role I couldn't have told you then, nor can I now.

In the space (no pun intended) of six hours and four earth orbits, we watched South Africa's Springboks beat the All Blacks in the rain at Newlands, admired Tiger Woods lifting yet another trophy, caught spectacular images of Somali pirates boarding a cruise liner, and had our first meal away from mother earth.

I found myself thinking that if we could see so much of what is happening around our planet, certainly God could too.

I said as much to Mark.

With his gaze solemnly locked into mine, elbows on knees and chin resting on clasped fingers, he quietly asked me, ' Then why doesn't God reach out to the growing shambles which is now our planet? Tell me that, please sweetheart.'

I remained silent, unsure, and Mark continued with what seemed to me infinite sadness, ' If there is a God in all this, where is He? Why His stony silence?' In reply I raised my eyebrows and shrugged my continuing uncertainty.

Our return to earth at O.R. Tambo outside Johannesburg was exciting but otherwise uneventful, and our lives continued much as before.

Matthew

One day, only a few months after completion of Bolters Burrow, Mark and Mary asked us to meet them there one sunny Sunday morning.

Intrigued, Hayley and I arrived early, only to find they'd beaten us to it.

Together we entered, made coffee, and brought out deck chairs to take in the wide-angle view of False Bay, from Gordon's Bay to the left, round to the long finger of Cape Point on our right.

Mark started the ball rolling by telling us they were going to sell their home in Constantia, and asking if they could live in Bolters Burrow while they looked around for a property in the area between Kalk Bay, Simonstown, and beyond.

'We really do want sea views, and this side of the peninsula is definitely our favourite. Yours too, isn't it?' Mary finished brightly.

We both knew, though, that this wasn't the real reason for them wanting to move.

Hayley and I were quite startled, and Hayley asked them what had made them want to move from one of Cape Town's most upmarket suburbs so suddenly.

We could see both were somewhat embarrassed to answer, and the reason was soon made evident by Mary.

'You know in Constantia we have that large troop of baboons which have become emboldened to jump on stationery cars, and even scare people into giving them food?'

'Well, you've told us about them, and of course we've seen them occasionally on visits to you. They're called the Constantia Contingent by most of the locals, aren't they?' Hayley asked in some bewilderment, and I said surely baboons being around wouldn't make you want to sell a home you love so much.

'Don't forget there are troops of baboons on this side too!' I added in helpful warning.

But their minds were obviously already made up.

'The final straw,' Mary answered with utter conviction, 'was when we came home a few days ago, and were surprised to see the kitchen door ajar. On looking in, we saw with horror the big Alpha male baboon sitting on the kitchen table nonchalantly munching a loaf of bread, while Wacca, our Australian cattle dog, sat on the floor in front of him wagging his tail and begging for some. Seeing us, that horrid great baboon got nonchalantly off the table, defecated contemptuously on our spotless kitchen floor, and casually walked out the door with the remains of our loaf tucked under one arm, followed hopefully by Wacca still wagging his tail.'

I'm ashamed to say my involuntary reaction, spontaneous as it was, did not go down well with the Lincolns. My guffaw of laughter frightened birds in flight, and must have been heard down in the town and naval dockyard way below. Even Hayley was a bit taken aback, though I thought I detected traces of a smile hovering in her eyes and on her lips.

When I was able to speak once more I apologised profusely, but visualising again the scene of dog on floor begging from baboon on the Lincoln's kitchen table brought on a fresh paroxysm of mirth, so I got up and stumbled away trying to control myself.

Finally under some semblance of order but weak at the knees, I returned to the group, where Hayley, Mark, and Mary were making suitable plans for the move without me, and with only limited input from me a deal was struck, and our friends would occupy the Burrow for six months to see how they really enjoyed this side of False Bay.

'Certainly the best possible assessment of its fitness for purpose,' I said in the plan's endorsement, redeeming myself somewhat before we went down to and across the main road for calamari and chips at The Salty Sea Dog.

Mark

Mary and I soon established a great early-morning routine at The Burrow.

Up before sunrise, we walk down the hill and across the main road to a small stretch of usually, at that time of the day, deserted beach.

On balmy mornings, the majority, as the sun rises over mountains across the bay, picking out Kalk Bay fishing boats returning with the night's catch, and trickling through branches of trees where we sit and drank coffee from a flask, as sea slowly slithers on sand amongst rocks, we never cease to be amazed at how it can all change so quickly.

On other windy, wintry early mornings, pummelling waves crash relentlessly on those same rocks, and spume is blown up into our faces. Seagulls career screeching around the sky, and we're never quite sure whether they're having the time of their lives, or regretting getting airborne.

Whichever sort of start to our day it happens to be, though, we're always thankful for all of the changes to our lives we've made since we left Chicago.

After a brisk climb back to The Burrow healthily raises our heart rates, and a languorous shared shower is followed by a quick multi-fruit breakfast, our sixteen-hour days get properly underway.

The first sign that something truly momentous could seriously affect our planet and therefore our lives came via Captain Luke Logan aboard USS BISON in the Somali Basin.

It was a Sunday morning, bright and sunny. A morning when it felt particularly good to be alive, full of life and hope for greater understanding, not a time for bad news.

The Captain told us, on a direct security phone link, that the American Government had sent a secret advisory to all security arms world-wide, indicating that a vast shower of meteorites were heading towards our planet, of which a large number were destined to strike our planet over the course of several days, within seven days.

The advisory went on to say that the likely repercussions of numerous strikes on earth and sea by huge meteorites, though largely only guessed at, would doubtless be catastrophic in themselves, in addition to which, vast, destructive tsunamis beyond imagining would devastate most areas of our planet less then sixty-plus metres above current raised sea levels.

On top of that these gigantic movements of seawater, many covering hundreds of miles of ocean every hour, would bring unusual pressure to bear on fault lines under the oceans, rippling across continents, causing earthquakes unknown in such numbers and intensity since time began, and triggering global volcanic eruptions.

The advisory ended with the bleak words—This will be the end of all our lives as we know them. It may well herald the end of our world.

Citizens will be informed of emergency measures as and when they are formulated.

In God We Trust.

Of course we immediately contacted Matt and Hayley, jointly deciding this was the signal for once-in-a-lifetime decisions of GO or STAY. GO for ARK-2 to take us into space, STAY to take our chances in the burrow.

Matthew

Agonising for an hour, we Drapers decided on space, the Lincolns on staying earthbound.

Doubting Thomas wanted to know if it really was a good idea to be heading into space, or already there, with a cloud of massive meteorites coming in the opposite direction.

I had too many other things on my mind to consider options over which we humans had no control, and told him so.

Within 36 hours, my family, Luke Logan and his wife Cindy, his former Chief Engineer John Flanagan and wife Jackie, Chris Justes with partner Maralyn Demage, were in space orbit aboard our ARK-2 named *Alpha-Omega*.

Mark and Mary Lincoln had been adamant they would rather remain on earth, and the Burrow was stocked with a year's survival requirements.

What followed was beyond belief, a nightmare.

As predicted, over a period of 72-hours or so, time no longer seemed to matter any more, we witnessed asteroid strikes, earthquakes, volcanic eruptions and tsunamis, many travelling in different directions and crashing spectacularly into one another.

Without doubt, what'll remain for ever etched in my mind was watching lights being extinguished in villages, towns, and whole cities along swathes of continental coastlines.

The Pacific Rim of Fire lived up to its name.

Washington, London, Beijing, Moscow, Mumbai and Lahore were obliterated by nuclear devices, recognised as such by Captain Luke Logan, realising instantly Leila bint Hammadi had taken immediate advantage of world-wide panic to get her five operatives in position to activate their plans early.

The combinations of all these caused ever-growing clouds of thick, dark volcanic ash clouds mixing with nuclear fall-out quickly obliterating our ever-changing views of our planet's surface, and spreading deadly toxic rain worldwide.

In overwhelming awe at what we witnessed, communication even amongst ourselves on board ARK-2 was desultory and fearful at best.

Of course we wondered how the Lincolns were faring in the Burrow, much like us, we imagined, cowering in our cocoon up here, no sign of life in the outside world.

An eerie communications silence had begun almost immediately, and continued as we circled endlessly.

Chris Justes and Maralyn Demage spent all their time huddled together.

After a period of six or seven weeks, the dark clouds covering our planet began to thin and disperse noticeably. Through odd gaps we could make out nothing but ice and snow on sea and land. As the clouds finally cleared, apart from individual storms, it became apparent there were no recognisable signs of human, animal, or plant life left on our planet.

When Brett, always an avid player of word games, holding pen and paper, tapped me on the shoulder while signalling his mother to come closer too, we were quite stunned at what he'd written.

Eight words in capitals.

CHRIS	JUSTES	MARALYN	DEMAGE
JESUS	CHRIST	MARY	MAGDALENE

The three of us looked in amazement. Were these merely word-games? Anagrams? Or what?

Were Chris and Maralyn as we knew them, members of Y.E.A.S.T. like us, of which Chris had been Chairman and Maralyn Group Secretary since the group's inception, playing some game, or had they actually known all along that what was happening before our eyes was The Bible's Armageddon?

But before we could even begin to discuss this, there was a shout from Luke Logan monitoring the screens showing our planet below.

We gathered at his shoulder, to find he had finally discovered an area in central Australia encompassing Alice Springs and Ayers Rock, now known as Uluru, that appeared to be the only place on earth not covered in ice or snow.

From space we could detect no sign of human, animal, or plant life in the vicinity, but as our resources for survival on board had dwindled to almost nothing, and it appeared our landing controls were fully functioning, our crew quickly and unanimously decided to leave space immediately and take our chances of ultimate survival back on earth.

Hopefully God was with us, and He was on our side!

Our descent and touch-down proceeded without a hitch, and we exited our ARK *Omega-Alpha* soon after local sunrise.

What was immediately apparent as we stepped back onto *terra firma* again were human footprints on the bare earth, but no visible sign of them, and casting our eyes about wonderingly and with trepidation, we saw the surrounding eucalypts had been totally destroyed.

We were greeted by an eerie silence. No sound, no signs of movement.

Luke was the first to assess the situation. 'We must find these people, they can't be far away. Our resources are desperately low. Perhaps we don't see anyone because they're afraid of who we are, so they're hiding.'

A sentence in the Bible's book of Revelations came to my mind right then. "He that overcometh shall inherit all things."

Had we, from ARK-2, *Omega-Alpha,* just inherited Alice Springs? Australia? What was left of the world? Had we been guided by God all along without understanding? Were Chris and Maralyn really Jesus and Mary Magdalene, the Second Coming?

Was there some pre-ordained connection here?

An excited shout jerked me back to reality.

Two-hundred and fifty metres away were huge, undulating, earth-coloured domes, of what at first glance appeared to be plasticised material, stretching away into the distance. The footprints led in that direction.

It was Luke Logan who knew precisely what this was.

'That's Australia's Eden Enterprise, based on Cornwall's Eden Project in the U.K. I saw a programme about it on T.V. not long ago. Bloody amazing how it's survived, I have to say. With luck there should be millions of plants in there, hundreds of varieties, meaning food a-plenty unless everything's died, of course, but I'm willing to bet that's what the people whose footprints we've just seen live on.'

'Perhaps,' Chris Justes exclaimed excitedly, 'that's where some of them are as we speak,' and set off at a fast walk towards the structure, others straggling behind, uncertain what to expect next.

Suddenly the ground Chris Justes walked on started to judder and quake while a thunderous roar filled the air around him.

'Jesus Christ,' he exclaimed, as a gigantic, heaving, tsunami-like wave of earth, rock, swaying trees and shrubs reared higher and higher and rolled rapidly towards him, its high crest of foaming dry red dust stretching as far as he could see from side to side.

Screams from in front and then behind stopped him in his tracks.

As its base reached him, he felt himself whisked Heavenwards, and gasped 'Almighty God, here I come,' as all the breath was sucked out of his lungs.

Back Page

This parable reconciles Christianity's Bible with the notion that Evolution is God's plan, despite which the World as presently exists could end in our lifetimes.

Notes on the Author

Scott Millar has lived all his life in a Southern African country, where he has farmed, been an hotelier, held a Pilot's Licence, and Administered a Retirement home.

For the last few years he has avidly studied Christianity's extremely chequered history, and followed advances in the science of Evolution.